THE GIFT

THE GIFT

TRIPURARI SHARMA

Seagull Books
CALCUTTA 2008

Seagull Books 2008

Cover design: Sunandini Banerjee

ISBN-13 978 81704 6 335 1

Published by Naveen Kishore, on behalf of
Seagull Books Private Limited
26 Circus Avenue, Calcutta 700 017, India

Printed in India by Leelabati Printers
P54 Ananda Palit Road, Calcutta 700 014

The 'Other Person' enters as Friend, a bat in one hand, bouncing a ball on its flat edge. He moves about the stage but concentrates all the while on the ball, counting softly—'Forty, forty-one, forty-two . . .' When the ball drops and rolls on the ground, he runs after it and picks it up. Smiles in relief and looks at Children. Then he looks around the stage as if missing someone. Peeps into the wings. Catching Children's attention, he turns to them.

FRIEND. Was anyone here? I mean, before I came. (*Children answer, 'No'.*) No? You mean you haven't seen Gaurav? There, late again! Always the same story. (*Looking up as if at a balcony, he calls out*) Gaurav! Gaurav! (*To Children*) No sign of him. How can anyone take so long—when he knows he has to come to play. I always make it first. Takes me an hour—come from school, throw off my bag, shoes and socks, change my clothes, wash my hands, gulp down lunch, then lie down with my eyes closed. That's how it should be. But I toss and turn, grunt and sigh so much that they let me out. A harmless little trick—that's all. They've got to sleep, you see, while I play my game—and mind you, it's my favourite one—yes, cricket! You guessed it. Enjoy it too? Well, the game's such! And when you score run upon run—singles, doubles, fours and sixes—crossing the boundary and going still, leaps and bounds—especially with your own bat in your hand—do you have one? Your own? Isn't it great? I've got mine too, a bit worn out and old but as they say, old is gold. And even though it's a little small—(*Embarrassed*) I've suddenly grown tall, you see . . . Never mind, here goes a four and here a six! (*Mimes a few hits*)

As if he had been waiting to make a dramatic entry, Gaurav enters holding a new bat. The musical score of the film Lagaan *plays in the background.*

GAURAV. Just as a single stroke of Bhuvan's won the match, so will I hit a six! The winning six! And India'll be at the top! Because of me and my bat. My new bat!

FRIEND. Look, Gaurav's so happy! And why not? He's got something after three months. Three months of mumbling, grumbling, shouting and screaming. But now all that's forgotten. With the bat in his hand, his face is all smiles. Well, when you get something, something you really want, then naturally you're not going to pull a long face and be miserable. I mean a gift, whatever it is, is a pleasant surprise and if it's of your own choosing, then . . . Now how did you feel when you got it—one fine day, all wrapped up in shiny paper and waiting to be opened by you? What was it—a dress? Chocolates? (*Discussing with Children*) A toy car? A pencil-box? Something that made you jump for joy? Like him, there? He really needed that new bat! Rohit would make him field every day, 'Don't let the ball go out of the boundary,' he'd say and keep playing, refusing to be out. The grand bat was his, so he made the rules. And when Gaurav's turn would come, Rohit'd look at his watch and say, 'Oh no! Time for my computer class. You can have your turn tomorrow, don't mind!' and scoot. Just like that. Tomorrow never came, of course. (*Looking at Gaurav*) New?

GAURAV. Brand new. Can't you tell? See the shine!

FRIEND. Where'd you get it?

GAURAV. My father got it. You know the shop just outside Nehru Stadium? They have the latest smartest stuff. That's where. I think Sehwag also buys from there.

FRIEND. Wow, what luck! Let me see. (*Moves closer*)

GAURAV. You want to have a look at it? (*Moving away and holding the bat high in the air*). There! Seen it—clear and proper? (*Walks off*)

FRIEND. Not like that. Let me hold it.

GAURAV. Hold it? Your hands're clean?

FRIEND (*wiping his hands on his shirt*). Oh, come on.

GAURAV. Anyway, you've seen it already. (*Moves away*)

FRIEND (*enviously*). It's very nice.

GAURAV. Nice and fine
Smells like pine
Bat number one
Makes run after run
Four and six
Never in a fix
Play and win
Yeah, that's him!

Stands centrestage—all set to bat. Friend isn't too happy.

FRIEND. So, who's going to bowl today?

GAURAV. Who's got the new bat?

FRIEND (*gets his point but still tries*). Look, I'm a fast bowler.

GAURAV. Go on, as fast as you can. My bat'll set you right.

FRIEND. I spin too.

GAURAV. Googly or spin,
Never will you win,
There lies the rat
For my bat's a cool cat!

FRIEND. Let's see.

Aims and throws the ball, Gaurav hits it well. Friend is taken aback; bowls again. Gaurav hits it just as well as the first time.

FRIEND. Careful—I'm giving a Harbhajan throw! Don't you hit too hard! (*Bowls*)

GAURAV (*hitting*). I'm just playing, the bat's the wonder!

The ball rolls away quite a distance.

FRIEND. Look, the ball's going too far. (*Panting, picks it up and bowls again*)

GAURAV. Far or near, the bat's in gear. (*Hits*)

FRIEND. Not fair! If you're going to aim so wide, then call Gauri to field.

GAURAV. I'll call her but you keep going. (*Hits again*)

FRIEND. Look, I can't run so much. You go get the ball.

GAURAV. Who's the other team?

FRIEND. All right, but (*moving to the ball*) it's not fair—bowling and fielding at the same time!

GAURAV. Gauri'll come. Till then . . . (*Friend returns unwillingly to his place*). You'll get your turn, of course. (*Friend bowls. Gaurav hits.*) There! See!

FRIEND (*on the way to fetch the ball, tripping and falling*). Aaah—a pebble's stuck in my foot! (*Clearly pretending*)

GAURAV. Oof! Come on—don't spoil the fun! (*Moves to take a look at the injury*)

FRIEND (*wincing and hiding his foot*). It's okay. Let's carry on.

GAURAV. See, when Gauri comes, she'll be at the boundary. You be in the middle areas and when the shots fall close by, I'll pick up the ball and pass it to you. Happy? I'm not in your team, but still. (*Turning to Children*) After all, we're friends—so rule or no rule, it doesn't matter.

FRIEND. Good idea! (*Starts playing with the ball on his own*)

GAURAV. Come on then.

FRIEND. Let her come first.

GAURAV. Oh yes. (*Looks up tentatively at a window*)

FRIEND. She's there.

GAURAV. I know, I know! (*Looking at the window again*) Gauri, come now. (*To Friend*) There! Let's play.

FRIEND. But—

GAURAV. A friendly match while she's on her way.

FRIEND. She's still upstairs.

GAURAV. Oh, she'll come. Come on—

FRIEND. But she hasn't budged.

GAURAV (*in the direction of the window, urgently*). Gauri!

FRIEND. She's not moving.

GAURAV. No, not an inch.

FRIEND. As if she's stuck with glue or something.

GAURAV. Gauri, come! We're waiting! Time to play!

FRIEND. She's not listening.

GAURAV. Of course she is. Gauri, sister dear, can you hear?

FRIEND. She looks fed up!

GAURAV. No, no. She's just wanting to feel big and important. Wait, let me try—Gauri, we'd be really happy if you'd care to step down and join us. (*Bows exaggeratedly*) Welcome!

FRIEND. She's showing her thumb. Sticking out her tongue. She's teasing you.

GAURAV (*sticks out his thumb at the window and makes faces*). Uuu-tututu . . . dadada!

FRIEND (*amused*). She's turned her back! Two hoots for all your faces! (*Laughs*)

GAURAV (*stops abruptly*). Hey, she's gone! (*In a tone of finality*) So she's not coming.

FRIEND. Maybe she's got homework.

GAURAV. That's over and done with.

FRIEND. Maybe mother's given her some work.

GAURAV. At play-time? Never! She won't do it.

FRIEND. So that's that. Now let's switch. Pass me the bat and you bowl. (*Moves to pick up the bat*)

GAURAV. Why—I'm not out yet!

FRIEND. But that's how we play now.

GAURAV. It's not done! (*Appealing to Children*) Hasn't bowled me out yet, has he? There—they know it too.

FRIEND (*to Children*). But he's batting so hard—I can't go running all over the place.

GAURAV. That's because I'm so good—my bat's so good.

FRIEND. See—they don't agree.

GAURAV (*insistently, to Children*). You do, don't you? You know the rules of the game.

FRIEND. Yeah, but I must have a team. You call Gauri, then it'll be fine.

GAURAV. You know she won't come.

FRIEND. Try again.

GAURAV. No use. She's sulking! Spoilsport! Just because I've got a new bat and she hasn't got her cycle. It's not my fault.

FRIEND. But she'd asked for one.

GAURAV. Papa said no and she gave up. That's not the way to do it. You've got to go on and on and on.

FRIEND. So go on and on and call her.

GAURAV. No point. She's sulking. Jealous. Always behaves like this. I never do it—never! For Rakhi, papa gave me fifty rupees—to give to her of course. And I did too. She tied the rakhi and I gave her the money, just like that—didn't tease her or make her run or bargain for chocolate. Then, on Ramnavami, she went house to house with her friends and guess how much she made? At least thirty-five bucks. How she was showing off. But I didn't mind. I never mind. She does.

FRIEND. You also followed her, door to door.

GAURAV. One or two houses. And they gave me pudding on a plate with a spoon. No coins. But I didn't mind.

FRIEND. Your cheeks puffed up.

GAURAV. No, never, not even when she got a new dress.

FRIEND. You got new clothes too.

GAURAV. Yeah yeah, but I could have—if I wanted to. Be jealous, I mean. Who can stop anyone from being that? But not me. Tell me (*asking Children*)—is this nice? The way she's behaving? Should one mind like this? Just because somebody else gets a gift? (*Children tend to agree with him*) See, they think it's not done. Should not be done. Let her be with her sighs and sulks. I'm not going to try and make up. She'll see.

FRIEND. Then she won't talk to you.

GAURAV. Let her not.

FRIEND. She won't help you with your homework.

GAURAV. Who cares? I'll do it much better on my own than with her poking—

FRIEND. And no playing together.

GAURAV. So? I'll play by myself.

FRIEND. So you don't want her to.

GAURAV. Did I say so? (*Startled, turning to Children*) Never. I'm the one calling her again and again. 'Come on, let's play.' But I know she won't come.

FRIEND. Sure?

GAURAV. Yeah, because she's not in the right mood.

FRIEND. And what is the right mood?

GAURAV. When she's happy.

FRIEND. And when's that?

GAURAV. That? When she tops in class. When her friends ring up. When it rains. When there's good food. Sweets, you know—she loves them. And when there's gossip—someone teased someone and she talks about it and laughs. Then two little holes form in her cheeks. Mummy says, There, Gauri, your dimples are showing again. And she loves it and laughs again and the dimples go in and out and in and out and in and out. (*Laughs, enjoying her laughter*)

FRIEND (*looking stealthily at the window*). She's at the window again.

GAURAV. Looking at me?

FRIEND. Well, she's standing there.

GAURAV. Facing this side?

FRIEND. In a way.

GAURAV. Well, that's something.

FRIEND. Really?

GAURAV. Let's make her laugh.

FRIEND. If you want to.

GAURAV. A song! Silly and witty—she'll love it. (*Holding the bat as a guitar, he starts to sing. Friend joins in towards the end*)

Gauri, hey Gauri
Never be sorry!
Come and play
That's the way
That makes the day!
Gauri, hey Gauri . . .

(*To Friend*). Is she looking?

FRIEND. Well!

GAURAV. Laughing?

FRIEND. Can't say.

GAURAV. Smiling?

FRIEND. Maybe—

GAURAV. But she's there.

FRIEND. Yes—

GAURAV. Looking at us.

FRIEND. No, sideways.

GAURAV. Then why're you dancing! For whom? (*Exhausted, turns away*)

FRIEND (*trying to cheer him up*). Let's play something. A game. Something more interesting

GAURAV. She'll think we're having a good time without her—ignoring her. We don't want her. That's what she'll say—

FRIEND. So we'll keep calling?

GAURAV. Her? Never!

FRIEND. No, not like that. But say . . . if we make a train and it's going—

GAURAV. And you can hear the whistle blow a hundred miles—a hundred miles away! (*Mimicking a train whistle*) Kooo! Kooo! (*Loudly, to an imagined crowd of passengers*) Ladies and gentlemen! The train is about to leave. All passengers on board, please! Here we go!

FRIEND. Blow the whistle.

GAURAV. Koo . . . koo. Attention please. This is the last call—ladies and gentlemen. (*To Friend*) Is she coming?

FRIEND. She'll come—carry on.

GAURAV. Has she moved?

FRIEND. Come, let's start—

GAURAV. Koo! And here we go, up the track, past the hills—to your right is a cornfield, to your left a meadow of mustard flowers—yellow and green to greet the queen. Above us is the sky with a bird—a huge bird—and here we turn and cross into a valley, over the bridge, above the river, koo . . . (*Turns and sees no Gauri*) Where's Gauri?

FRIEND. How do I know?

GAURAV. You said—!

FRIEND. Did I?

GAURAV. Hey, look, there's the enemy—Fire! (*Uses the bat as rifle*)

FRIEND. They fire back—dishum! Dishum!

GAURAV. Aah! (*As though shot*) Here I go . . . Help! Help! Somebody—anybody—help! Water . . . Water! (*In a low voice, to Friend*). She's looking?

FRIEND. No. Not any more.

GAURAV (*exhausted*). Aah . . . she's J, not G. Miss Jealous G.

FRIEND. Maybe if—

GAURAV. Forget it. Let her ride her high horse. Just because she hasn't got a cycle. Well, I can't get her one, can I?

FRIEND. But your bat—you could give her that.

GAURAV. My bat? This bat? Something else, anything but not this.

FRIEND. Why not?

GAURAV. Well, something else can also be nice. And she may like it more. (*Turning to Children*) No?

FRIEND. What other thing?

GAURAV. Anything. Maybe a pretty card.

FRIEND. Let's make one. Quick.

GAURAV. Well, my drawing's not great. According to her, it's the pits.

FRIEND. So? You're just huff-puff-and-bluff.

GAURAV. No, no, I could buy her one if you think that's ok. You know, one of those that says 'sweet sister, sorry sister' and a face pops out—like that! (*Sticks out his tongue*)

FRIEND. You're teasing her.

GAURAV. She may think so.

FRIEND. So then that's out.

GAURAV. Maybe some other gift? Something really nice?

FRIEND.You're serious?

GAURAV. You bet!

FRIEND. Without a penny!

GAURAV. I've more than a penny, much more, More than a handful, if you please.

FRIEND. Really?

GAURAV. Not in my pocket, of course. But there's the money-box. It's quite full.

FRIEND. It better be—for the gift, I mean.

GAURAV. I could buy anything under the sun, it's so full.

FRIEND. And you're ready to spend it?

GAURAV. Any day.

FRIEND. Well, get it then.

GAURAV. Here?

FRIEND. Wherever.

GAURAV. It has a shining twenty-paisa coin. Pure gold, I tell you.

FRIEND. Get it then.

GAURAV. Now?

FRIEND. What are you waiting for? Christmas?

GAURAV. I suppose I could get it.

FRIEND. Let's see it then.

GAURAV. I mean, I can.

FRIEND. Sure.

GAURAV. Should I, then? Well, if you say so—(*Leaves*)

FRIEND (*picking up the bat*). Wow, what a grip! One in a hundred! (*Gaurav rushes in*) Got it? So fast?

GAURAV (*snatching away the bat*). Hey! My bat! (*Rushes out again*)

FRIEND (*to Children*). Can't bear anyone to touch it! What d'you think—will he get the money-box or run away? Well, it's tough to get anything out of a money-box. It's yours all right but the moment you actually want to spend from it, all hell breaks loose! So I never could! Have you ever managed to open your box and buy something with your saved-up coins? Ice cream? Chewing gum? Soda? Earrings? A new shuttlecock? A movie ticket—(*many of these are suggested by Children and Friend repeats them aloud*)—fantastic!

Gaurav returns.

GAURAV. It's not possible. My mother's in the same room.

FRIEND. Holding the box!

GAURAV. She'll ask, What are you doing with it? I can't get it.

FRIEND. Say you want to put money in it.

GAURAV. She'll ask, Why outside?

FRIEND. Then forget it. And forget the gift as well.

GAURAV. No, no, never.

FRIEND. Then you've got to get going.

GAURAV. Bring the box, you mean? Should I? I can, you know.

FRIEND. Then do so. (*To Children*) Ask him to go and get it.

Children ask Gaurav.

GAURAV. Will I? I might just. Actually—

FRIEND. We're waiting.

GAURAV. I'll just bring it. I'll go. (*Pauses for a moment as if waiting for a change of opinion*) Right. (*Runs behind the curtain*)

FRIEND. What do you expect this time? Money-box or another excuse? (*Children give their opinion*) And what if he—

Gaurav enters huffing and puffing.

FRIEND. There!

GAURAV. Impossible! Really impossible.

FRIEND. Come now—we knew it! Didn't we? (*Glances at Children*)

GAURAV. You couldn't have. Now Gauri's in the room. And my mother. And the box in the middle. Between the two of them. No way!

FRIEND. Oh, come now. Can't you just—

GAURAV. Just what?

FRIEND. Just—get them out of the way.

GAURAV. Out of the way? (*Thinks*) That's not tough. Meow!

FRIEND. Meow?

GAURAV. Meow! Meow! Meow! Could try that! Wait—give me a chance! (*Yells*) Mom, look, the cat's in the kitchen. The milk's gone, all gone. (*Runs behind the curtain, screaming*) None left for your evening tea!

FRIEND. That's how Gaurav created a ruckus. His mother and Gauri rushed into the kitchen. The coast was clear and we reached the moneybox!

Lights change. Gaurav and Friend enter from behind the curtain—tiptoe, eyes alert. The moneybox is under a stool. Gaurav moves toward it.

GAURAV. Shut the door—look out through the window.

FRIEND. Hurry up, get it out! (*Keeps a look out as Gaurav dives under the stool*) Got it?

GAURAV. No. Not yet.

FRIEND. Quick!

GAURAV. Pull! (*Friend is puzzled*) Pull me out. I'm stuck, you fool!

FRIEND. Oh I see . . . (*Pulls him by the feet. The stool falls over. Gaurav emerges with the box wrapped in a cloth.*) Never mind—now let's see what's inside. (*As Friend moves towards Gaurav, he changes direction*). Now what?

GAURAV. Shh, I'll show you something. Come. (*Takes him to a corner, close to Children. Friend brings the stool forward. Gaurav unwraps the cloth, then gently puts the box down*). Ha! This is the secret wonder box!

FRIEND. Take out the money.

GAURAV. I am, I am. (*Slowly opens the box and takes out a smaller box. Opens that and takes out another one. Opens that and takes out a coin*). Here, here's some.

FRIEND. Not enough.

GAURAV. More? (*Takes out two more coins and drops the earlier one back in the box*). Enough.

FRIEND. But this is better! (*Grabs the box and opens it, many coins drop on the cloth*.)

GAURAV. Wow! So many coins—don't touch . . . My mom says it's not good to go near other people's money. It's not good manners.

FRIEND. I see.

GAURAV. But never mind, I'll show you—see this twenty-paisa coin. Pure gold. Very precious. (*Puts it away—picks up another*) This my father gave me. On my last birthday. Can't be spent. (*Puts it away*) Look—this has Bhakra Nangal on it. Very rare. Must be kept. (*Puts it away too*) And this—this has Mahatma Gandhi on it and this one has Nehru—quite a collection!

FRIEND. So, no gift—

GAURAV. Why not?

FRIEND. Then be prepared to spend the rest.

GAURAV. Yes, yes, but not this . . . This is from ninety-seven, this ninety-eight, ninety-nine, two thousand, two thousand and one, two, three . . . One each for a year. I collect them, you know, and I'll go on collecting them. Forever and ever.

FRIEND. But the shops won't be open for forever and ever.

GAURAV. Yeah yeah, I'm on my way.

FRIEND. Here, keep the lot! (*Stuffs Gaurav's pocket with the remaining coins*)

GAURAV. Show me your hand—the other one. Raise your arms, turn around. (*Claps his hands*)

FRIEND. No, I kept nothing! They're watching. They wouldn't have let me.

GAURAV (*to Children*). Thanks. So I'm set! Well, wish me luck! I'm off for now. Bye. (*Leaves*)

FRIEND. So that's how, his pockets stuffed with coins, Gaurav went off to the market to buy a gift. (*Moves to exit, stops*) What do you say—will he get one?

Children respond. Music. Friend exits

Enter Gaurav—hands in pocket—as if in a market, looking around at the shops and signboards. A little nervous but trying to hide it.

The 'Other Person' appears from behind the curtain. He is now a seller of sweets, pushing a trolley. He will change into various shopkeepers in the course of the 'market' scene. Right now, he appears to be frying something, his right hand making circular movements while with the left he shoos away imaginary flies.

SWEET-SELLER. Round and round
Sizzle and sound
Wheel in wheel
With a golden peel
Bright as the sun
A small sweet one
Juicy crispy crunch
Munch at lunch or brunch.

GAURAV. Jalebis! Juicy and delicious. Hot and fresh. Just the thing. Don't you think? How many will do? One? No, I mean one kilo—is that too much? Why, I'm also there. Won't she share? I mean, that's all right with gifts. It's allowed. No?

SWEET-SELLER. Round and round.
Sizzle and sound.

GAURAV. Bhaiya, please, I want—(*stares at his left hand*) Hell, flies!

SWEET-SELLER. Oh come on—they're everywhere.

GAURAV. But they're not supposed to sit on the sweets.

SWEET-SELLER. They do. They come and go.

GAURAV. But that's not right for sweets. Children love sweets and children, as they tell us in school, are the future and if the future falls ill—

SWEET-SELLER. Go on—you snob, teaching me about sweets! (*Moves away*)

GAURAV. Well, I can't give her this, can I? First sweets, then sweet pills to follow. There've got to be some rules. As mom says, First good for the tummy, then for the taste.

The 'Other Person' has gone to the corner and, with mild alterations with an imaginary shopkeeper, sets up a fruit-chaat stall.

FRUIT-CHAAT-SELLER. Tasty taste
Not made in haste!
Sour dressed in spice
Like the sayings of the wise
Apples and grapes
Fruits of all shapes
Chopped up fine
Lemon and lime
All yours for a dime!

GAURAV. Ah! Cucumber and sour stars sprinkled with thick brown spice!

FRUIT-CHAAT-SELLER. Fifty-six powders if you please!

GAURAV. Gauri will jump for joy!

FRUIT-CHAAT-SELLER . As they say—sweet, sour and spice! Three in one slice! Wakes up the taste buds—cleanses the eyes!

GAURAV. Just the thing I want.

FRUIT-CHAAT-SELLER. A big leaf bowl or a small one?

GAURAV. I won't eat here. It's to take home.

FRUIT-CHAAT-SELLER. Brought a container?

GAURAV. Won't this leaf bowl do? Or will the juice trickle away?

FRUIT-CHAAT-SELLER. Well, people do take it—

GAURAV. It won't lose its taste, will it?

FRUIT-CHAAT-SELLER. Let it reach home first.

GAURAV. That's not a straight answer, is it? Suppose the spices drip away and only bits of tasteless fruit are left? She's not ill in bed. (*Sighs*) But it looks nice and oh, the smell of spice! (*Looks longingly at the 'fruit'*)

'Other Person' moves to another corner and sets up a kulfi stall.

KULFI-SELLER. Someone likes
When summer strikes
Hot high at noon—
Here comes a boon
Cool cool kulfi cool
Creamy-n-puffy wool
But chilled as ice
And white as rice
A lolly you pick
All set on a stick!

GAURAV. Not bad, eh? (*Going to Kulfi-seller*) How much, sir?

KULFI-SELLER. Two, four, six, eight, ten.

GAURAV. Give me one for two. Not two halves! (*To Children*) Just to taste. (*Carefully takes out some money and pays*)

KULFI-SELLER. Out of the cast, hold it fast! (*Hands Gaurav a kulfi*)

GAURAV. It's milk all right, and nutty too. Flavour of rose and—hey (*looking from hand to elbow as if the milk is trickling down*)—it's melted already!

KULFI-SELLER. Cool-cool boon-boon but be quick and eat it soon! (*Moves away*)

GAURAV. Good I didn't take it for her. It would have vanished in the sun and I'd be left holding the stick. Like a clown. Cool cool—fool fool! (*To Children*) You knew that would happen, didn't you? Well, so did I, but . . . That was greedy of me, you think? But how to be sure until you try. I know better now. And for just two rupees! The usual ones—not the special coins. Those are safe here. Not to be used. Unless,

unless of course it's absolutely necessary. (*Shows and stuffs some more coins away in his other pocket*)

'Other Person' has by now arranged some toys on top of a trolley.

TOY-SELLER. What a joy
To have a toy!
Holding in your hand
Something so grand
That glitters and shines,
Laughs and whines,
Stands and glows
When a trumpet blows! (*Blows a trumpet*)

Gaurav picks up a car and starts playing with it. The Toy-seller smiles and shows him another car and a truck. Gaurav rubs the wheels against his palm, then runs the truck on the ground. The Toy-seller brings the cart forward. Both play.

GAURAV. Show me more! (*Picking up a plane from the trolley*) Wow! (*Pulling out another one*). And this one's even bigger that—(*Pretends to fly it. Lands it on the floor, then scrabbles about the trolley, searching for more toys*)

TOY-SELLER. Hey—hey—!

GAURAV (*paying no attention, picking up a helicopter*). A helicopter that really flies! High and still higher.

TOY-SELLER. First, tell me what kind of toy are you looking for?

GAURAV. Me? Nothing. It's for my sister.

TOY-SELLER (*a bit annoyed*). Why didn't you say so? I've got just the thing you want. (*Dips his hand into the trolley and takes out a few packets. Gives them to Gaurav*)

GAURAV. What's this?

TOY-SELLER. Tea set, kitchen set, room set, doll set.

GAURAV (*staring at the packets*). No fun—are they?

TOY-SELLER. Depends. Some love them.

GAURAV. These! (*Opens the tea set—Cups, saucers, a teapot*). They're pretty all right. (*Turning them over*) But they don't move. Not like this. (*Runs a car over the cups*)

TOY-SELLER. Hey—hey careful, son. This's delicate stuff.

GAURAV. Yes, but what do you do with it? From the teapot into the cup—no, no. First cup and saucer, cup and saucer on a tray. Then the sugar-pot, milk-pot, teapot. It's tricky—you've got to fit them all. (*Arranging a tray*) Gauri can do it. I've seen her. But I don't think she likes it because it always leaves her in a bad mood, grumbling and fuming.

TOY-SELLER. But you've got to begin from the start. Polly put the kettle on! And for that you need a kitchen set to make the tea. Here, look at this! (*Takes out the kitchen set from the packet and places it in front of Gaurav*)

GAURAV. Ugh! She hates that!

TOY-SELLER. But they're lovely toys. Once you love them, you love the job too.

GAURAV. She'll yell at me.

TOY-SELLER. Oh no! Not when she makes tea and everyone says, How nice!

GAURAV. How nice! Yeah, I know that. First, she'll make tea for Mom and Mom'll say, 'Such a good child'. Then Mrs Chopra'll come and Mom'll say—'You know, Gauri makes excellent tea. Will you make some for your aunt, dear?' And of course Gauri will, for one and then for two. They'll say, How nice, and Mom'll smile and Gauri'll blush. First for Mrs Chopra. Then Mrs Mathur. Then Mr Gupta. Then Mr Sen, Mrs Sen, Miss Kothari, Miss Ahmed, Miss Choudhary, Mrs Singh Mr Singh—huh! When'll she play with me? She's got to play!

TOY-SELLER. These are imported. Tried and tested.

GAURAV. That's not the point. You don't understand. I want . . . I want . . . Now, let me see—ah, that might be—(*Takes out a doll*)

TOY-SELLER. This doll? Or the big one? There are many.

GAURAV. Yeah, that one. (*Holds the doll. Enjoys holding it and isn't awkward*) Ah, she closes her eyes! Sleeps . . . Then wakes up!

Wide awake! Her hands and legs move too. Gauri also has a doll. Her arms go up straight. Then Gauri pulls them down. Makes her sit. (*Seating the doll in his lap*). No don't overdo it. Don't talk too much. Pull your skirt down, socks up. All that boring stuff she passes on to the doll. (*Suddenly lifting it high above his head and throwing it up into the air*) See!

TOY-SELLER. Hey—hey—

Catches the doll and passes it to Gaurav. He throws it back. It goes to and fro between them. Then Gaurav throws the doll up and lets it drop.

GAURAV. We were playing like this when the bulb broke and Mom hit me once and Gauri once. Then we had to stop playing in the house. So I went out to play. And the doll looked at me. Gauri stood by the window, doll in hand, fiddling with her hair. (*Tone softens. Looking into the distance*) Maybe taking out lice (*Grows quiet, then suddenly turns to the Toy-seller*) No, she bathes the doll also. Then, once she kept her in the sun to dry. Along came Flashy, Verma-Uncle's dog, and ran off with the doll between his teeth. I rushed after him—Uncle, your dog's taken our doll, Uncle! Then Uncle also chased Flashy and got it back for us. And the doll was hurt. Gauri cried so hard. Then Papa told her, 'Throw it away. I'll get you a new one'. And Gauri said, No not a doll. Get me a cycle. Papa said, 'We'll see'. Then she went to her bag and took out the doll and started wiping her tears. I mean, Gauri was crying but she was wiping the doll's eyes. I don't know whether she wants a new doll. I mean she loves her but she also said, No. Maybe the old one was nice for her but a new one . . . (*Lost in thought*)

Meanwhile the Toy-Seller has picked up the doll and moved off. Turned away from us, suddenly he opens an umbrella. The 'Other Person' is now a Showman, wearing dark glasses, inviting people to aim and shoot at tiny objects dangling from the edges of the umbrella.

SHOWMAN. Aim high or low

Reap as you sow
Be best and brave
For victory you crave
Come try your might
With a target in sight
Shoot well and fire
Three rounds on hire.

The words have their impact on Gaurav and, though doubtful and despondent, he asks.

GAURAV. And where, sir, is the prize?

SHOWMAN. Many a prize. Of all shapes and size.

GAURAV. Show me.

SHOWMAN. Later. If you win. (*Gaurav seems to move away*) But I'll tell you what I have. Rubber, pencil. Biscuits. Hand-soap. Hanky-box, and the great prize: shampoo!

GAURAV (*stopping and turning to Children*). Shampoo! Now that's something worth trying for. What do you say? She can use it and her hair will become all silky-silky. I'll say, See, Gauri I've won a wonderful shampoo for you! She'll be so thrilled? Yes! I'll take a shot. Tell me how.

SHOWMAN. Two rupees for a round of three. (*Hands him the gun*)

GAURAV. Oh, so big and heavy. Never mind. When one wants to do something, one just does it. What'll I aim at?

SHOWMAN (*pointing to a small bear dangling from the umbrella*). The bear.

Gaurav tries to focus. Walks up to the bear. Holds out his hand.

GAURAV. Hello there Mr Bear. If you weren't as small as a bug, I'd give you a nice big hug.

NARRATOR. Don't you go closer, lad. Shoot if you can!

GAURAV. That's not tough! I can win all of these.

SHOWMAN. From the line. (*Pulls him back*)

GAURAV. Oh oh, don't stuff up, please. (*Breaking loose and moving closer.*) Yes. Yes. Now (*Showman holds him back. Gaurav shoots. He misses. To Showman*) No? Missed? (*Looking at Children*) Well, I need just one prize. So it's good to practice before actually doing it. Next?

SHOWMAN. The giraffe. (*All set to hold him*)

GAURAV. Now let me see. (*Sitting, changing angles*). The neck's all wrong. For a baby giraffe—too long. (*Looking up*). Oh that's you, not him. Move away, please. Yeah, that should do. (*Taking aim*) What do you say to that?

SHOWMAN (*flatly*). The last turn. The Duck.

GAURAV. Duck for Luck. Well that's all I want. And I'm going to get it too. Voila! (*Aims again. Showman holds him back*). Yes?

SHOWMAN. No.

Gaurav is crestfallen and Showman moves on.

GAURAV. I knew it. His gun has a slant and it's so heavy. Look at my hands. Well, all that glitters is not gold. Suppose I did win the shampoo and suppose I did give it to Gauri and suppose she did wash her hair with it—then suppose all her hair fell out?! She'd be bald—imagine that! Good I didn't win! You know, this is all local stuff. I can't take such a gift, can I?

The 'Other Person' has left the trolley and returned with a bamboo stand (made like a tree) with bangles, trinkets, ribbons dangling from it.

BANGLE-SELLER. Spring is in season
So let go of reason
Give up all gloom
Like a tree in bloom
Colour and flower
You must shower
A bangle on the wrist
A ribbon hair-twist
Here hang the earnings
As a merry bird sings!

GAURAV. Clang-clang go the bangles. And ribbons hang at all angles. That orange one looks bright.

BANGLE-SELLER. It is.

GAURAV. And the blue one?

BANGLE-SELLER. To wear to school.

GAURAV. Not that. Show me the red and the yellow.

BANGLE-SELLER. Red and Yellow. Never be mellow.

GAURAV. One red and one yellow, how's that?

BANGLE-SELLER. Brightest in sight. Don't know why people wear the same on both sides.

GAURAV. So I'll have to choose too. And how much for one side?

BANGLE-SELLER. A metre.

GAURAV (*holding out his arm*). That big?

BANGLE-SELLER. Should be.

GAURAV. Red and yellow or white. (*Looking at a bangle*) Look at this green. Give me this one.

BANGLE-SELLER. That's a bangle.

GAURAV. Show me! (*Sits under the trinket tree, relaxed and enjoying himself*)

BANGLE-SELLER. Here, be careful . . . (*Gaurav takes the bangles. Holds them. Looks at them, enchanted. Then, one by one, he puts them on. First on one arm. Then on the other*) Ah—this is something. (*Moves his arm up and down, sideways although not effeminately. He shakes one arm vigorously, then the other one. Holds one against the other. Then puts on more. Holds them in his hands too and shakes them. Enjoys the colour, the sound*) It's like music.

BANGLE-SELLER. There are bindis to match, Shilpa's, Neeru's, Kalpana's. (*Shows him some*)

GAURAV. And Gauri's?

BANGLE-SELLER. The same, of course. High quality.

GAURAV (*sticking a bindi on his forehead*). Does it suit me? I'm sure it does. No? Never mind, it's good fun all the same.

BANGLE-SELLER. So will I put away the ribbon?

GAURAV. No no, wait. I'm taking those. They're for Gauri—

BANGLE-SELLER. There—

GAURAV. Well, let me see. (*Coming to Children*) It's all right then? A good job done? Just the colour of the ribbon. Help me choose.

BANGLE-SELLER. We also have hair-bands.

GAURAV. Hair-bands?

BANGLE-SELLER. In all colours. Latest.

GAURAV (*looking at them*). They're bright too. Then Gauri can keep her hair open. She likes that. But the point is: she has to plait her hair. She can't keep it open—it falls all over her face. It's too thick, actually. Left open, the look doesn't quite suit her. Her head looks like a beehive. And she looks like—guess what?—an angry goddess. I told her so. It made her more angry. And then Mom comes, oil in hand, and pours it all over her head. And it begins—dhap dhap (*mimes the mother oiling and plaiting Gauri's hair*) dhap-dhap-pat-pat. And Gauri says, Aah, ooh, aah! Mama stop' (*Hits the air lightly*) 'Keep still or they won't be straight!' 'Dhap-dhap-pat-pat!' And when the plaits're done, Gauri looks like an angel . . . a shiny moon face with a flower on either side. Mom really sets the ribbons nice. And when she nods, the flowers nod too and when the head goes side to side—so do the flowers. (*Smiles*) Really pretty—even I think so. But Gauri'd rather leave it open. So tell me: what should I take? Hair-band or ribbon? I mean, I like the ribbon but she'd like the hair-band. What I like? Or what she likes? What I like or what she likes? What I want or what she wants? How I'd like her to look? How she'd like to . . . I like . . . She likes . . . What should it be? Both? That's too much. Ok, shall we do heads-and-tails? (*Taking out a coin*) Heads it's her, tails it's me. So? (*Changing his mind*) No—tails it's her and heads it's me. No, no, I mean heads is ribbon and tails is band.

BANGLE-SELLER: O band-master! Stop harping on my band! (*Picks up his things and leaves in a huff*)

Gaurav is left in the midst of confusion. Then, as Children point out (*or he remembers*), *he rushes to return all the objects, hurriedly peeling the bindi off his forehead.*

GAURAV. Here—all your things! I'd have pay if you hadn't remembered. Gosh! (*Sits down with a sigh*) Now what? It's just getting tougher. That-this-this-that—it's endless. Who'd have thought getting a gift meant so much? Honestly, between you and me, I've never really bought a gift before. Mom gets me stuff to pass on to friends and all, but this is like being on a merry-go-round. Round and round—and not so merry any longer. Simpler to let her choose herself. I can't rack my brains any more. (*About to leave*) Unless you can? Any ideas? (*Invites suggestions*) Teddy bear? Watch? Schoolbag? Book? Clothes? Too many ideas! I'd rather go and tell her, 'Look, I'm willing to get you a gift. I mean, I've decided to get you one, if only you choose it yourself!'

As he turns to leave, the 'Other Person' enters as a clothes merchant. His arms are stacked with rolls of cloth and yards of fabric hang from his shoulder, are draped around his waist, and so on.

MERCHANT. Now you've come to the right shop, Children's Evergreen Clothes and Shoe Corner! A must for every buyer!

GAURAV. Well, if you have something for—

MERCHANT. If? We most certainly have, just the right thing—the one you're looking for. (*He rolls out a yard of cloth on the floor. Gaurav rushes over for a look and sits down on the ground, feeling it for himself*) If it's not that, then it's this. (*Rolls out another yard of cloth on the other side of Gaurav*). Or this! (*Gaurav moves to the new roll. Gets entangled in the fabric*).

GAURAV. No, no, not so much. Just a little bit for my sister. (*He tries to break free but the fabric is wrapped around him. He rolls in the opposite direction to disentangle himself*)

MERCHANT. Ah, here we have a nice pink, soft pink, bright pink, rose pink, lotus pink, candy pink, baby pink. (*Peels off shades of colour stuck to his costume and throws them at Gaurav*)

GAURAV. Pink's not her colour.

MERCHANT. No? Then maybe yellow is—light yellow, dark yellow, lemon yellow, glow yellow, mango yellow, mustard yellow, daffodil yellow, sun yellow.

GAURAV: No, it's too hot.

MERCHANT. Then here's just the shade to cool. Maybe blue's her hue—sky blue, ocean blue, navy blue, royal blue, teal blue.

GAURAV. Help!

MERCHANT. No? Then readymades! Here you are! Aishwarya Rai-style, Amisha Patel-style, Manisha Koirala—

GAURAV (*desperate*). That's not her name. You've got it wrong.

MERCHANT (*taken aback*). Have I? Really? Maybe—

GAURAV. No more clothes. I'm off. (*Leaving*)

MERCHANT. Maybe you could try some shoes? (*The trolley is pushed out onto the stage and Merchant pulls it forward. On it are arranged various kinds of footwear—chappals, sandals, high-heeled shoes in silver and gold, school shoes, sports shoes, etc. The trolley stops in front of Gaurav. He looks at it and then at Children.*)

It's a rare collection
Something for the feet,
In cold and heat,
Cushioned for rest,
But try the test,
Go near or far,
On stones or tar,
Whether tiny or tall.
They'll last you all.

A small smile appears on Gaurav's face. He pushes the trolley closer to Children.

GAURAV. Aren't they nice? I'll take the silver one?

MERCHANT (*hands it to him*). It's a high heel.

GAURAV. Yeah! (*A bit fascinated by the heel. Placing it on the floor and putting his foot in*). Hey, she'll be tall, as tall as Mom! Then Mom can't scold her.

MERCHANT (*handing him the golden one*). This is a pencil heel.

GAURAV. Yes? What style! (*Putting his other foot in*). Ah, still taller. Almost as tall as Papa. Great. And when she'll walk, she'll look down like this. Like a giraffe. (*Laughs and walks, then suddenly trips and falls*). Ouch! That hurts. Like falling down the stairs. So dangerous. No, not this!

MERCHANT. You've got to know how to walk.

GAURAV. Not her. Maybe that one's better. No? (*Looking at Children*). The sandal's better? Those gold things, dangerous stuff, no way she'll like that. But with a sports shoe she can walk, she can run, play—it's soft, it's warm. (*Touching and feeling the shoe*)

MERCHANT. Try this one.

GAURAV. She'll wear them and run, fast, fast, faster. Faster, faster, faster, faster, fastest! Ahead, ahead of everyone, ahead of me. (*Pauses, then looks at Friend*). Do you have one in another colour?

MERCHANT. Just one piece. (*Takes the shoe from Gaurav*)

GAURAV. One piece then? (*Lets the Merchant go away. A bit uneasy*). I won't give up! I'll get something for sure. But what?

As he moves, a basket appears from behind the curtain. He stops to look at it and pulls it out. The 'Other Person' comes along with it. He has changed his hat.

GIFT-MAN. Excuse me—may I help you?

GAURAV. A gift, I want a gift.

GIFT-MAN. Here . . . all here. This? (*Takes out a flower, long pencil, purse. Gaurav shakes his head to all of them*) Books? (*Takes out a few from the basket and spreads them out*)

GAURAV (*looking attentively at the books*). Why didn't I think of it before? Now I've found exactly what I was looking for.

GIFT-MAN. Storybook?

GAURAV. No. No.

GIFT-MAN. Comics?

GAURAV (*thinking*). Tch . . . tch—

GIFT-MAN. Novel? Encyclopaedia? Dictionary? Science-fiction—

Gaurav doesn't seem satisfied with any. Suddenly his face lights up.

GAURAV. That one, the one with noodles on it!

GIFT-MAN. Cook-book? Nice, really nice. Good choice.

Gaurav grins and grabs the book and flips through the pages with interest.

GAURAV (*moving to Children*). Look at this. Every meal's a party. Indian, Chinese, Continental. All in a ladle and pan, chowmein, chopsuey, Hakka noodles, spring rolls! Chicken–cheese cutlets, mushroom and baby-corn soup, caramel custard, jelly, gulabjamuns.

Now this is yummy.
For tongue and tummy
Every dish a feast
Lucky we're born to eat.
Just boiling and frying
Little bit of trying
When the smell does excite
The tooth to bite
What a moment to be
For Gauri and me!

'Other Person' has by now resumed the role of the Friend—and is standing behind Gaurav. He now taps him on the shoulder.

FRIEND. So this is for Gauri!

GAURAV. She'll gobble it up.

FRIEND. You're expecting her to cook? (*Looks sharply at Gaurav, who feels a bit caught out and embarrassed but shakes it off*)

GAURAV. No, no! Of course not. (*Looking at Children*) Did I say that? Never.

FRIEND. But somebody has to.

GAURAV. I see. Somebody. Can be anybody. (*Looking at the book with pictures*). Maybe even me. What's there? I'll do it. It's not so hard.

FRIEND. You!

GAURAV. Why not?

FRIEND. Ever seen a kitchen?

GAURAV. I'll get to see one now.

FRIEND. All in one go?

GAURAV. Well, why not? What's the big deal? I just migh!

FRIEND. Look who's talking!

GAURAV. The one who's going to be walking.

FRIEND. We'll see. (*Leaves*)

GAURAV. Now to business. We've got to do it now—to prove a point. So what'll it be? Cheese mushroom peas—too many things. Baked aubergines? What's that? Looks like brinjals—that's cheating. Like calling a chappati a full-moon wheat plate. I want something straight and simple. Sandwich? Too dull. Cabbage stripe Kandhari pomegranate potatoes? Too stuffy. Something small and sweet . . . sweet . . . Here we are . . . Puddings. Yes, she loves those. Egg pudding—break shells and chocolates . . . and caramel . . . Carrot . . . gajar ka halwa . . . grated carrots . . . grate? Oh grate (*realizing what it means*) no, no, too clumsy. Almond–fig pudding . . . Bread pudding . . . gram-flour pudding . . . Potato pudding, sweet-potato pudding, pumpkin pudding . . . pudding of puddings . . . walnut–currant–rice pudding . . . semolina pudding . . . Ah, also called sooji ka halwa. Aha—semolina sounds grand and it's yum. Plus, it's Gauri's favourite. And it's the smallest recipe, only fifteen lines. No fancy names either. Manageable. Say we give it a try?

Friend returns with the trolley, now arranged like a kitchen counter with a gas stove. He ties an apron onto Gaurav.

FRIEND. Ready?

GAURAV. Yes ready, one-two-three-and-start! First—things you need: a frying pan. (*Picking up a bowl and a frying pan—stares at them*) Which is what? (*Children point out or Friend does*) This? (*Keeps it to one side*) Now (*confused*) spatula . . . What?

(*Picks up a spoon, a frying sieve and a spatula. Then realizes what he needs*) Ah, this! You need good GK to be in the kitchen. Now, semolina (*Opening a box*) What's this? (*Tasting*) Baking powder—ugh! What's semolina like?

FRIEND. A bit rough.

GAURAV (*opens another box, tastes the contents and spits*). Then this is it. Now, 200 grams. How much is 200 grams?

FRIEND. 200 grams is 200 grams

GAURAV. What's your weight?

FRIEND. Forty-five kilos.

GAURAV. So one finger is how many grams?

FRIEND (*perplexed*). How can you weigh a finger?

GAURAV. Say, this is 50 grams. (*Putting Friend's finger on one of his hands*) And in the other I take a fistful. (*Taking some semolina*) Yeah, it feels the same. So this is 50 grams, one, 50 grams two, 50 grams three, 50 grams four. (*Pours four fistfuls into the pan*) 50 grams. (*About to continue but either Children or Friend stop him*)

FRIEND. Hey, no more.

GAURAV. Okay, so that's 200 grams done. Now ghee or clarified butter. (*Puts a scoopful in the pan*)

FRIEND. Look in the book.

GAURAV. Book! Ah yes. . . the page . . . the page . . . where's the page? (*Flips through the book*)

FRIEND. Keep moving it.

GAURAV. Moving? Yes, moving. (*Still flipping through the pages*)

FRIEND. Forget the book—look at what you're cooking. Move that.

GAURAV. Oh, yes yes! (*Tosses away the book and moves the pan a bit*)

FRIEND. No no, move the sooji, you fool! It'll burn.

GAURAV. Oh, oh! (*Quickly stirs the sooji in the pan. Then stops, looks at Friend and smiles in a superior way*). Hah—how? Tell me, how will it burn when there's no fire? Relax! You've got to be brainy and bright to make a dish so light. (*Lights the stove*) Now we're set. (*Peeps into the pan*) Wow, the ghee melts and becomes like water. You know, the glacier up there must be like this. Softly, softly, snow's melting.

FRIEND. Careful, it may burn!

GAURAV (*stirring*). The smell! The pudding smell! Has it reached you? Boy, this is fun.

FRIEND. Water, water, pour some water!

GAURAV. Ah, here! That's the waterfall. (*Pours in a jugful*) Up comes the smoke and steam. It's just a dream.

FRIEND (*reading from the book*). Keep handy half a cup of sugar and nuts.

GAURAV. Sugar! That I know for sure. (*Opens a tin*) One. Two. Three . . .

FRIEND (*stopping him*). Enough. Now nuts.

GAURAV. Nuts? (*Opens a box*) One almond, two cashews, three raisins—enough? (*Puts them in*) Look, bubbles like lava frothing out of the earth. Like raindrops dancing in the yard. Ready, dream pudding. You're in the making. (*Taps the spa-tula against the pan, then stirs with it round and round while chanting*)

Pitter patter pitter patter
Don't you dare chatter
Something's in the making
Count the time it's taking
One two three four five
You can see it come alive
If close to the stove
In kitchen's own grove
You get a booking,
To know what's cooking
Like it's fun to watch
From the field a match
Hold on the suspense
It's getting a bit dense.

Thick and fluffy
Red hot and puffy!
Keep off for it's hot
But deep inside the pot
Something's gurgling, bubbling
Murmuring and mumbling
Looking like pudding.
Setting like pudding
By Jove it's the pudding

Both are gleeful and excitedly looking at the wonder cooking in the pan.

FRIEND. It's done.

GAURAV. Thick and smooth; spongy and brown. (*Looking up from the pan to Children*) We made it.

FRIEND. But the taste of the pudding's in the eating.

Gaurav looks sharply at Friend. Then takes a spoonful and puts it on a plate. Passes it to him.

GAURAV. Hey wait! (*Takes out a nut and puts it back in the pudding*). Now, taste. Tell me, how's it?

FRIEND. Should I? (*Hesitates, then puts a spoonful in his mouth. It is hot and his expression registers that something is wrong*)

GAURAV (*growing pale*). Something's wrong? It's a flop. I knew it. Nothing works. You try and try but it just won't happen like you want it to. It wasn't semolina. I felt it. Now it all goes to waste. (*Takes off his apron*). Sorry friends. It's a pity, though. We tried.

FRIEND. But it's really good. (*Gaurav stares in disbelief*) It tastes like real pudding!

GAURAV. You're kidding. (*To Children*) Remember the face he made?

FRIEND. It was so hot!

Gaurav stares at Friend in disbelief. Friend lifts him up in joy.

GAURAV. But was it edible?

FRIEND. By all standards—yes!

GAURAV (*relieved*). So it's ready—my gift. You think it's ok? (*Takes out a spoonful and is about to put it on a plate when he looks at Children*). Want some? (*Takes the pan and scoops out some for them. Then stops*). Is it anything like pudding? Will Gauri like it? Do I go now and surprise her? (*Holds the pan with delight*) Wish me luck so she may smile! So long! (*Walks through where Children are sitting with the pan and pudding*)